Published by Inhabit Media Inc.
www.inhabitmedia.com

Inhabit Media Inc. (Iqaluit), P.O. Box 11125, Iqaluit, Nunavut, X0A 1H0
(Toronto), 146A Orchard View Blvd., Toronto, Ontario, M4R 1C3

Design and layout copyright © 2014 Inhabit Media Inc.
Text copyright © 2014 Rebecca Hainnu
Illustrations copyright © 2014 Hwei Lim

Editors: Neil Christopher and Louise Flaherty
Art director: Danny Christopher

We acknowledge the financial support of the Government of Canada through the Department of Canadian Heritage Canada Book Fund.

We acknowledge the support of the Canada Council for the Arts for our publishing program.

Printed in the United States of America

Library and Archives Canada Cataloguing in Publication

Hainnu, Rebecca, author
        The spirit of the sea / by Rebecca Hainnu ; illustrated by
Hwei Lim.

ISBN 978-1-927095-75-1 (bound)

        I. Lim, Hwei (Illustrator), illustrator II. Title.

PS8615.A3853S65 2014   jC813'.6   C2014-905066-6

The Spirit of the Sea

by Rebecca Hainnu · illustrated by Hwei Lim

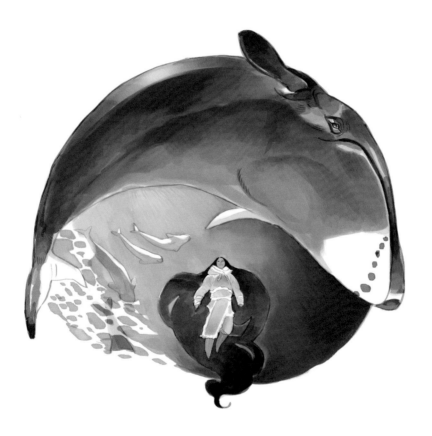

INHABIT
MEDIA

Long ago, when animals were able to speak with humans, there lived a beautiful young woman called *Arnaq*. She had lovely brown eyes, smooth, tanned skin, and long, shiny black hair. She always wore the most beautiful *kamiik* and parkas, and she lived happily with her *ataata*, travelling across the land. Ataata spoiled Arnaq, because her *anaana* had died when she was very young.

When Arnaq grew up, young hunters from far and near came to woo her. But Arnaq's stubborn heart could not be moved, and she scorned them all and sent them away. Despite her ataata's pleas, Arnaq refused to marry and be enslaved to a lifetime of hard work.

When spring arrived, and the sea ice broke up, Arnaq and her father moved their camp to the shore. There they lived a peaceful and solitary life.

One day, a fulmar that was disguised as a handsome young man arrived at the camp. He was called *Qaqulluk*, and he was a powerful shaman.

Qaqulluk sang an enchanted song, and the song pierced Arnaq's stubborn heart:

"Your *qulliq* will always be filled with oil, and your pot with food. You will have the best pelts for clothes, and the softest caribou hides for blankets. My tent is made of the best skins. Come with me and be my wife."

Arnaq could not resist such wooing, so they left together and travelled over the vast sea in his kayak.

8

At last they reached Qaqulluk's land. Arnaq had endured a long, tough journey, only to discover that her new husband had lied to her. Her new home was made of disgusting fish skins. It reeked of an unbearable smell. The tent was full of holes, which let in constant cold drafts and snow. Arnaq found pieces of tattered walrus hide sewn together to make a dreadful blanket. It was nothing like what Qaqulluk had promised. There were no soft pelts. All she had to eat were the fish that the other fulmars brought to her. Eventually, Arnaq succumbed to complete depression.

Arnaq regretted her decision to follow the fulmar. Foolishly, she had scorned many young human hunters. In her pride, she had declined the chance at an ordinary, happy life.

In her sorrow, she sang meekly, "*Ajaajaa*, Ataata, if you knew how miserable I was, you would come and get me. You would take me away in your boat. The fulmars stare at me with mean eyes and scream loudly—they scare me. Although they bring me food, it is always the same stinky fish. Ataata, if you love me, you will come and take me away from this wretched place, ajaajaa."

Whispering, she finished, "I need to go home."

A whole year passed. All winter long, Ataata felt a strange need to go check on Arnaq in her new home. When spring arrived, and the vast sea ice finally opened up, Ataata travelled to visit his only child. When he arrived, Arnaq greeted him with much warmth, although she was very distraught. She told him everything, and begged him to take her away. Outraged, Ataata wasted no time, taking her swiftly away on his boat. Witnessing this, the flock of fulmars went to warn Arnaq's husband, who was out fishing for her dinner.

When Qaqulluk heard that Arnaq had left him, he and the other fulmars flew with great speed and caught up to Ataata's boat. The flock of fulmars, screaming and encouraging Qaqulluk to seek revenge, swarmed around the boat. Furiously, Qaqulluk screamed, "Give me back my wife! She left freely with me!"

Ataata, still angry with Qaqulluk, yelled up at him, "You tricked us, you treacherous bird. You do not deserve such a beautiful human wife."

Qaqulluk and Ataata exchanged more angry words. Suddenly, gusting winds began to blow with each flap of Qaqulluk's wings, and waves rocked the boat. Qaqulluk caused a very frightful storm. The little boat was thrown around in the waves like a rag. Ataata's anger was replaced with absolute terror.

In an effort to save his own life, Ataata decided to offer Arnaq to the fulmars. He thrust her overboard.

Arnaq seized the side of the boat. Crazed with terror, Ataata yelled at her to let go, but still she held on. When she refused to release her grip, Ataata took a long snow knife and cut off the first joints of her fingers. Arnaq's fingertips fell into the water, turning instantly into whales. Her fingernails became whalebones.

Still she held on with all her might, but the sharp knife fell upon her fingers again. When the remaining joints of her fingers fell into the water, they turned into seals, and swam away.

Arnaq disappeared beneath the surface.

The flock of fulmars shouted in victory and turned away, assuming that Arnaq had drowned. The storm subsided.

Ataata, who was utterly ashamed, floated away in his little boat.

And as Arnaq sank deeper into the sea, the sea mammals swam protectively around her, following her small body as it was pulled slowly to the bottom.

From that dreadful day onward, the sea changed Arnaq. She became the spirit of the sea, and is now known as *Nuliajuq*.

It has been said that her home at the bottom of the sea is built of large stones and whalebones. Sea mammals obey her, because they were once a part of her.

When humans disrespect the land or the sea, Nuliajuq becomes displeased. She calls her sea mammals back to her home—keeping them out of reach of human hunters—and causes great storms.

Since the day that she was taken by the sea, the only way for humans to appease the fearsome Nuliajuq is to send a shaman down into her lair to soothe her. Only then will the waters become calm and the sea mammals return to their hunting grounds.

As for the fulmars, Nuliajuq has taken away their ability to speak, so that they may never deceive another innocent soul. To this day you can hear them wailing in regret.

Afterword

This book is only one of many versions of this story told by the Inuit.
Depending on the region in which the story is told, the woman in the story
is called by different names, including Nuliajuq, Takannaaluk, Taliillajuuq,
Arnajuinnaq, Aningapsajuukkaq, and Uinigumasuittuq. Whichever name
you know her by, she is often addressed as "Arnaq," the Inuktitut word
for "woman," at the beginning of the story. The father in this legend is
always nameless, and is only ever referred to as "her father." In this version,
"Ataata," the Inuktitut word for "father," is used as a character name, as is
"Qaqulluk," the Inuktitut word for "fulmar." In many Inuktitut stories about
animals, the character's name is often the name of the animal in question.

Pronunciation Guide

Inuktitut word	Pronunciation	Meaning
ajaajaa	a-ya-ya	A traditional musical refrain
Anaana	a-na-na	Mother
Arnaq	ar-nak	Woman
Ataata	a-taa-ta	Father
kamiik	ka-miik	Animal-skin boots
Nuliajuq	noo-lee-a-yook	A woman who never wanted to marry, and who became the spirit of the sea
Qaqulluk	ka-ko-look	Fulmar, a grey-and-white Arctic seabird
quilliq	kood-lik	A soapstone lamp that burns seal oil

Rebecca Hainnu lives in Clyde River, Nunavut, with her daughters Katelyn and Nikita. Her work includes, *Math Activities for Nunavut Classrooms* and *Classifying Vertebrates*. She is also the co-author, with Anna Ziegler and Aalasi Joamie, of *Walking with Aalasi: An Introduction to Edible and Medicinal Arctic Plants*. Her book *A Walk on the Tundra*, also co-authoured with Anna Ziegler, was a finalist for the 2013 Canadian Children's Literature Round Table Information Book Award, and was among the 2012 "Best Books for Kids and Teens," as selected by the Canadian Children's Book Centre.

Hwei Lim studied engineering, worked in IT and business consulting, and now draws comics and other stories. Recent published works include art for *Spera: Volume 1*, and the Boris & Lalage series. Hwei lives in Malaysia.